DEALS IN LOVE

AND MANY OTHER STORIES

SUMIT BHUYAN

ISBN 979-888555503-6

DEDICATED TOMY MAA AND PAPA

Contents

Acknowledgements

I am from normal family and I have faced a lot of obstacles in my life. But in this situation the people who helped me and for which I wrote this book...

I would like to thank Soumya Ranjan who has guided me every time in each step. He is one of the India's youngest writer and also helped me in writing this book..

I would also like to thank my father Mahendra bhuyan and mother Kiran bhuyan who always shower their blessings on me.

I would like to express my heartfelt gratitude to Sangita Mahapatra,Madhusmita Nayak

Amit Ranjan Bhuyan,Sasmita

Reliable Rakshi and Jaydev Sahu .

Thank you everyone for being with me and please guys give support to my first book

About The Author

Sumit Bhuyan is an entrepreneur from Jamshedpur. He loves writing shayari and he loves writing lyrics...He has his own organization known as The open minded in which his team used to promote talents and also he used to upload some interesting news.

He also organises events all across India in which many participate .He belongs from a Middle class family

ONE

DEALS IN LOVE

A cheerful boy from a lovely city of Jamshedpur (Jharkhand) was brilliant in aesthetics and was an average in academics ... Education system of India affected him severely as he choosed to learn archery but his parents forced to focus on studies and build up your career...His mother said " Padhoge likhonge banoge Mahan, kheloge kudoge banoge kharab"....Anil always refused and enjoyed his life and used to work upon what makes him happy.The journey started from a teenager who lives in Jamshedpur. Jamshedpur has always been one of the fastest growing cities in India which is developed and managed by TATA Group.

Known to be the Steel city of India, it happens to be the only City that doesn't have a municipality in India. The city of Jamshedpur has soul which keeps it very lively. People mainly fall in love with the liti Chokha of Jamshedpur.

People in the city hold happy go lucky nature. Arun was a cheerful boy who did his schooling from English Medium School, Vidya Bharati Chinmaya Vidyalaya. His dream was to start up a small business and then build company like Jamshetji Tata. He was very fascinated towards bringing new experiments and at last he used to break and spoilt things. Arun's dad worked as a supervisor in an automobile company and mother was a housewife. Arun parents struggled a lot to give him a wonderful life. Considering the financial condition of his family he took can admission in a nearby college. Arun join a tutor of Mr Jeevan who taught the pure Science students remarkably. Mr Jeevan's students never failed in any of the examination as he taught them very nicely . He was a very intellectual teacher and his teaching style is unique and different.

In his school days he heard about launching of mobile phones but due to Commercial conditions , was not able to bring one for him. His father was a supervisor and nearly earned 12,000 per month and he was supposed to carry out his expenses , his mother's expenses and his grandparents expenses and his too. In his college days all started with unexpected events.He was a introvert and mixing up with the bundle of college students made him feel uncomfortable. Though he was friendly in nature but the sudden change in the surrounding made him feel awkward. He was very fascinated seeing the mobile phone with every child was carrying to the college.

In his college days mobile phone was a trend among the students. Arun also demanded his parents that he also want to carry a mobile phone in his pocket.

His parents denied and Arun targeted his mother and charted his emotional drama to convince his mother. Arun's mother got sympathy towards Arun.

Arun's mother convinced Arun's father to buy a mobile phone for him.

After few days Arun was happy saying his new phone Samsung Galaxy M30 one which was launched newly in the market. Arun hugged his mother and father. Arun was warned that he should not misuse the cell.Arun also showed off to his friends by taking out his mobile phone 100 times from his pocket. One of his classmates complaint to the teacher about Arun's behaviour and Arun's mobile phone was snatched. Arun was told to bring his parents and only then he will be return the cell. Arun was scared and an idea hit upon his mind. New his building their lived an uncle who loved Arun very much. Arun thought to dress up that uncle like his father and carry him to his college. Arun tried to convince his uncle but the uncle scolded Arun because he wanted that Arun should not repeat the mistake again. The uncle accepted and went to Arun's School.

The professor after having a meeting with Arun's father(disguised uncle) gave Arun his ID card and warned Arun that if again he repeats this Mischief then he will be suspended....

Their was a foreign family which came to visit Jamshedpur. (Narration)My life changed forever the day I saw who was sitting inside our new car, It was a ghost, Katy's ghost! She was here to take revenge and there was nothing I could do.

That Sunday was really special to me as both my parents, Molly and Himesh were at home. They were normally quite busy and seldom had time to sit down and relax. I was scanning the newspaper for any fun thing we could do, when my eyes spotted the advertisement.

It was an advertisement for a midnight blue sedan. The specifications of the car were mentioned, with the address of the seller. But my eyes popped out when I read the last sentence, "Price whatever the Buyer quotes."

We were thinking of buying a car but the idea had been vetoed by my mother due to shortage of funds. I showed my father the statement and though he appeared reluctant, I knew he was interested too.

We set out soon after breakfast towards Mr. Hampton's home. He had a beautiful house but the car was breathtaking! After my father had driven the car and checked the working of its other parts. He took me aside to converse privately.

Both of us were clueless as to why Mr. Hampton would sell this gem at a dirt-cheap price. So we asked him the reason, in response his face lost its smile and in a grave voice , informed us that his daughter Katy had died in the car and still haunts it.

We obviously didn't believe his awkward ghost story but felt that we should buy the car. And now I understand that hasty decisions are the worst just like ours has become, a curse.

When we first drove the car home, even my mother who is not a car-fanatic liked it. But slowly weird things started happening. Once when me and Jake (my dog) were inside, the doors shut themselves and refused to open. When I thought that we would surely die of suffocation, at the last moment the doors opened and we crawled out, totally pale and breathless.

We had taken some photos of the car and though while clicking them no one was there, when we got them developed a faint outline of a girl could be seen. Sometimes when I would look out of my windows the car's internal light would be on. It felt as if it were calling me towards itself.

I had told my parents all this a number of times but they just refused to believe me. When I showed my mother the photos, she grew deathly pale. I asked her if she could see the girl sitting in the car but she just stood like a statue.

But today I have decided to face my fears. I will sit in the car and talk to Katy. I walked towards the car, opened the door and sat, waiting for her to strike.

"Oh Himesh what will we do? Didn't you see how he walked towards his bed, opened an imaginary door and is now sitting there."

"Molly stop crying, we'll take him to the hospital and he will be all right. Just like last time."

"Yeah, last time when he would drag an empty leash around the house and feed bits from his plate to the air. Didn't you see the photos he took? There was only an empty street in them."

"He will get better, we are taking him to the psychiatrist, right? He will be fine. Just because he is diagnosed with Schizophrenia, it doesn't mean he can't get better."

"But .....this is getting out of hand , first imagining a dog, then a car , and now this !"

"He will get better, Molly. He has to !"

From that incident he was too scared...

To divert his mind Anil's father narrated him a real life story.For the first time I saw him in the 'Elixir' Bar & Restaurant where I used to go often to give myself a chance to get rid of the angst of my life, which used to leave with two pegs. When a tall man with an attractive face opened his lilting songs they soothed my heart. I had sent my song requests to him many times, impressed with which he used to come to my table singing and included me in singing. Gradually we started having intimate talk. Of course, I weighed my words while talking with him in a subdued manner, but my heart longed for him and did not keep any check on my emotions. I was gradually being drawn towards him. Had he shown his love, I would have definitely reciprocated.

On that day, he sang this song "Wo Ladki Sabse Alag Hai" (That girl is quite different) in his attractive voice. It seemed as if I was sitting in the lap of that melody. As if he was propitiating me with that song. From the very heart, the dreamy bubbles rose and in a moment got burst. He knew only to throw pebbles into a calm pond of the heart. In a way, this indifferent human attitude towards me was making him a crazy person.

After all how many men are there in this world that show a genuine interest on a girl but only to turn into a selfish interest.

One day he suddenly came to me and said with great affinity. "Congratulate me and also feel sorry for me."

"Congratulations for what?"

"I have got the chance to sing a title track for a Daily Soap of TV; I am offered Rs 6 lakhs."

"Wow what a great break through … many many congratulations … but why sorry?"

"Sorry because, the music director will release my money only when I give him my G.S.T number. I am a singer, can sing the most intricate song, but I am not adept in paperwork. I take the help of a CA But before I complete all formalities more salt and pepper would fall on my wound of deteriorating finance."

"Can't you request him to make payments without documentation formalities this time?"

He is a number one cheat. Every one may not find him easy to deal with. He does not listen to anyone, but he puts his finger on everything. Once while buying mutton he showed his finger saying "not this, not that "while the butcher was chopping and in the process his finger came under the chopper. In spite of that he has not left the habit of fingering. He had fingered enough in my songs. I sang the song in 5 ways, only then he locked my song.

"Oh, is that so!"I reacted with a sincere response.

When a sentimental relation got established with him I asked in a subdued tone, "How much money do you need?"

"Rs.80 thousand!"

Overflowing with a polite smile, his face became the I Card of his gentleness. So there was no scope for any doubt. The very next day I drew Rs.80 thousand from my account and handed over to him. But from that time onward he was absconding. The reason for his absence was not even known to the Hotel Manager. The attempt to talk on mobile number, given by him to the Manager, also proved futile since his number was switched off.

"Why is he not coming? Has he fallen sick?"

A small part of my brain brought also this thought whether he was a cheat! But disproving my mistaken notion he turned up near my table after about 15-days, on a Friday evening, and began to say in a tone filled with regrets.

"I'm sorry; I could not meet you for all these days, being involved in the paper work. I have given my music director my G.S. T. and he has made the payment to me."

By saying this, he took out a cheque and showed me which was for Rs.6 lakhs. I got the happiness then for many things - happiness for my mistaken notion of him proving wrong, his happiness to receive the money and above all the happiness of his return to my life. I congratulated him jubilantly, but even my congratulations could not remove the depression seen on his face.

"Why are you looking sad?" I asked anxiously.

There is a bank holiday on the occasion of Eid tomorrow; the day after tomorrow is Sunday.... This cheque will not be cleared before Tuesday. I have to return your money too. I can pay you even on Tuesday but the Afghan Money Lender, from whom I had taken a loan of Rs.50 thousands is after my life saying, "Pay the money today or else I shall break open your skull."

His words scared me enough. This time again I told him that he would pay the money to the Afghan Money Lender by taking money from me. And on Tuesday, when the money comes into his account, he should return my money. I could feel from his eyes that he was filled with emotion, but was silent as there was no other alternative than to accept my proposal. I drew the required amount and gave him. He went away thanking me repeatedly. I immersed myself in this pragmatic realization that several days have elapsed after Tuesday. This time he has absconded not to be seen again. Time had brought some change in him. I got rid of all conjectures and realized one day that he was a cheat who, playing well with my sentiments, went away looting me.

I was an ethical hacker in a renowned IT company where the fat salary after meeting all my needs left substantial saving. Losing money was not a reason for my worry. What was disturbing me was the chicanery. The feeling for retribution choked my throat. I ransacked his account in every possible way through the internet. Even by my hacking skills, I could reach his account. I saw that he had Rs.8 lakhs in his account.

"You must have collected all this money shaving the heads of many people, like me. Look Mr. Rookie, what am I going to do with your ill-gotten wealth? "Thinking in my mind, I transferred all the money from his account to the account of a social institution. Now he had become an utter pauper.

The time had healed my wound. After 14 months, I recovered from this emotional accident and returned to my old colour and on that day, crossing the car parking, I moved towards the shopping complex, when in front of my eyes I saw a poor blind girl staggering and falling. I ran towards her and helped her to stand up. As soon as I leaned to pick up her materials which had fallen on the road I was rudely shaken to see the picture of Mr. Cheat in the broken photo frame lying there.

"This photo?" It is of my brother's photo. My brother had died on the same day last year by heart disease. Today, on his anniversary, I took out this broken photo frame from the blind shelter to fix it when I fell.

Upon hearing this my liver came to the mouth, but still I asked her, "Why didn't you get your brother treated in a good hospital?"

Brother did not want to leave me as an orphan in this world, therefore he had collected money, by running here and there, a big part of which has been hacked by a hacker. So he died without getting any treatment. By saying this, the girl left the deep breath of sigh.

I heard everything in silence with deep sense of regret as if I was completely dead and was carrying my own dead body on my shoulder. I was thinking whether he was a cheat or myself!

Days passed.....

Anil was now in class 10 and was preparing for his board exams. He was very mischievous his classroom and did a lot of such activities that annoyed his friends. He passed his board exams with average ranking. His parents were having the fear that he would fail but river not also so happy by seeing his marks but they were satisfied.

It was almost bed time, I was in the floor playing with my dolls on my right hand side was my brother playing with his UNO cards. It hit 9:00 PM. Once again it all started, I heard my aunt and uncle fighting yelling out about his drinking problems, I remember my brother hugging me tight. I can hear them cussing one to another.. I was scared my uncle was wasted.. tripping, screaming "I'm tired of this, I'm tired of you!" I knew this was not going to end well.

I closed my eyes tight holding my brothers hand, and shut a tear, he whisperer to my ear... "everything is going to be alright." It only took about two minutes to hear the phone being tossed to the other side of the room, I knew he would hit her, my heart started beating faster and faster as his voice started getting louder. I heard my aunt saying "This is when I hate you the most, this is when you turn into my worst enemy!" Does words scared me, I knew he was getting angry as she scream to him how much she hated him, as does words hit him on the softest spot he had, he became a different person when he was holding that bottle on his hand. He took a deep breath, and scream again "you are worthless, you don't understand me! Look at you no one will ever want you, no one will ever love you.."

My brother and I are in a corner holding hands saying our prayers for the nightmare to end, next we heard him slap her across the face, we wanted this to an end. We stepped outside trying to stop this my brother ran towards him.... I yelled at him "Please don't hurt us don't hit us.." Tears running down my face, my brother hitting him, kicking, screaming, biting him. My aunt yelled again " stop don't hurt them! Don't touch them.. you hate me!"

I saw him slamming her against the wall as my brother rand to hide. He started hitting her until she bleed, until she was weak enough not to get up. There was tears running down her face, she wasn't able to talk, I cover my eyes as he slammed her one last time. "I told you not to get in my business.. this is what you get, exactly what you deserve!" He yelled at her as he walked away. My brother in in the other side hiding his face, I rand towards him and said everything was to an end, we rand towards the phone, we called the cops. It was only a few minutes when they arrived, he was gone, no where to be found. As always in a small country they only took her to a clinic and they dismissed this case, there was not enough evidence...

I can only remember her recovering, it only took him a week to come back to apologize to try it one last time... She took him back she was scared and though without a man she was not able to make it, she needed his help to be the person she wanted to be. I didn't understand as a child her taking him back, my brother and I were always scared of him as the night hit we pray this wont happen again.. No one wants their child seeing violence, growing up with people hating each other teaching you that two grown people are always fighting..

My mother never knew about the argument, we were allowed to say anything. Can you imagine leaving your kids behind in the hands of two people feeling hate towards each other.. We should always remember what made us who we are. We can never forget the things that happen to us to teach us what life is, not everything is as it seems not everyone is born in a crystal box, some of us need to build our own box and learn how to keep it going up..

Anil was a handsome young man of 25. He had curly, close cropped hair with bushy eyebrows and light brown eyes, a pointed nose with a prominent cheekbone and a square jaw bone, giving his face a rectangular shape. He had a great physique and an attractive personality. He was a gold medallist in MFA painting. Besides, he had completed graphic designing and animation from a reputed computer institute. He worked for an advertising company and lived with his widowed mother Vidya in Nagpur. Life seemed to be very kind to him except that he had no luck in love.

Girls seemed to enter into his life and then abruptly exit like retreating waves from the sea. Though he was disheartened by his love failures, he was not averse to a romantic relationship with a girl. Whenever he was ditched by a girl, he consoled himself saying, " Perhaps, this girl was not meant to be your partner."

His mother was not at all pleased with his Casanova image. She advised him, " Fooling around with girls is like playing with fire. Be careful or you may get burnt." Anil pinched his mother's cheeks affectionately and said, " My dearest mom, relax! I have decided to lie low for a while. I assure you I won't go looking out for trouble. It's just that I worry about you. You need a daughter in law, who will do the household chores and take care of us. You can't blame me for my eagerness to get married. Most of my cousins are not only married, but also have children. Why should I lag behind?" His mother giggled but said nothing.

Days passed by, both mother and son were vigorous in their bride hunting but didn't get any suitable alliance. Anil posted his profile on the matrimonial site. He was disappointed to get lukewarm response from the girls. He wondered what was wrong with him? He was quite handsome, earned a decent salary and a house of his own. When he browsed through their profiles, he was taken aback by their sky high expectations. He kept on scrolling down the webpage to view profiles that could match his status. It was then, that a girl called Monica sent him a message. Anil was thrilled and he responded immediately. He was pleased to note that she didn't have any great demand. They shared similar views on subjects like education, politics, sports, marriage etc. They chatted for an hour and then Anil carried on with his daily routine.

The website chat resulted in friendship and gradually turned into love. Anil was ecstatic as he felt that he had found his true soulmate. He had already told her about his previous love failures and she had been a great sport to digest that information without any complaint. Their family background was quite different. He was a Maharashtrian and She was a Bengali. Yet their hearts were united. He introduced Monica to his mother who immediately gave her approval for their marriage. After a couple of days, he went to Kolkata where she lived, to seek her parents' consent. They also agreed to their match. Anil returned to his hometown feeling Victorious. His mother was very happy for him. Now, only the engagement and wedding date had to be finalized.

The twist in the tale was unavoidable, as Anil lost his job because of the company's closure. He called Monica and informed her that he was out of job. He asked her, "Now that I have told you about my unemployment, I want to know if you have any second thoughts about continuing our relationship. I won't mind if you prefer to opt out."

She replied, " How can you even think about it? I have been in love with you and not your job. I will wait for you till eternity. You will get a better job, sooner or later." His joy knew no bounds on hearing these soothing words from her. He was determined to get a good job within a short period. He kept on applying for job and attending the interviews but without any success. He was a fighter and wouldn't give in so easily to failure.

He was so busy searching for a job that he didn't bother to call Monica. Anil was still jobless.

He thought of çalling Monica and dialled her number. It was ringing but no one responded. He thought that she might be busy and would call back after seeing his missed call.

He waited for a week but she didn't respond. He called her again from his bedroom. She picked up his call this time and said, " Hello. I couldn't attend your call last week. I forgot to tell you that I am getting married next week to a boy from our own community. Since you didn't have any job, my parents opposed our marriage. I can't go against their wishes. I hope you understand the situation. Please don't call me anymore." Anil was always depressed thinking about that girl. He was totally in love with her but she never knew that the girl would cheat her so badly. Anil tried frequent attempts to commit suicide. Once while walking on the road he was very confused and was looking up to the sky. He was totally depressed and was thinking to end his life. Anils mother was waiting for him since morning and as didn't return home. Anil while walking was standing in the middle cross path and the truck was in rush to hit him but his friend Sunil saved him and kicked him down the road like a filmy drama. Sunil got hurt in his hand but he saved Anil's life. Anil started crying and shouted at Sunil saying "why you saved my life it was better dying by living such a depressed life. Sunil slapped Anil and took him to a garden named "Aam Bagan" and told him the reality of life.

Sunil told him " Suiciding is not the solution of a problem because who has cheated you will definitely be punished by God and also by the police but before taking some dangerous steps just think of your parents , what will happen to your parents if you die . Sunil told him " Suiciding is not the solution of a problem because who has cheated you will definitely be punished by God and also by the police but before taking some dangerous steps just think of your parents , what will happen to your parents if you die .

I am with you and I will help you out in solving every problem of yours but before that you have to promise me that you will not commit suicide anymore."

In a very low tone replied" ok brother ". Sunil tapped on his soldiers and dropped Anil to his home and was in a hurry to his house as he had a fight with his brother Anurag. Sunil reached home his brother shouted"Where did the milk go?" With empty Amul cartoon in one hand and fridge door in another.

"Back in the cow" Sunil replied and sat on the Sofa opening his laces of his new, sparkling white sport sneakers. His Fiancee Prerna has given him 4 months ago. Ofcourse Sunil was likely to enter a ladies toilet by mistake than a gym.

I am with you and I will help you out in solving every problem of yours but before that you have to promise me that you will not commit suicide anymore."

In a very low tone replied" ok brother ". Sunil tapped on his soldiers and dropped Anil to his home and was in a hurry to his house as he had a fight with his brother Anurag. Sunil reached home his brother shouted"Where did the milk go?" With empty Amul cartoon in one hand and fridge door in another.

"Back in the cow" Sunil replied and sat on the Sofa opening his laces of his new, sparkling white sport sneakers. His Fiancee Prerna has given him 4 months ago. Ofcourse Sunil was likely to enter a ladies toilet by mistake than a gym.His brother said "It's not a joke the carton was full and now I can't make a cup of tea" . Anurag shut the fridge in disgust , threw the empty carton in the dustbin and sat on the dining table chair staring at him." I will get another packet later" Sunil said.

Like a 12 year old kid Anurag stopped talking to Sunil .

Even though they lived together they communicated mostly through WhatsApp messages. Anurag WhatsApped Sunil even though he was at 7 feet away" I want to milk and now, I want tea".. Sunil while opening his shoelaces saw the phone screen and ignored the message. He again Messaged " please respond".

Sunil typed " Feeling tired, will sort out later".

Sunil sat on the dining table and told Anurag to serve dinner for him and he refused to do so and snatched the remote and started watching" Bigg Boss". Sunil was least interested in his f*** matter and rushed towards the kitchen and served the dinner for himself and after having it, he went to the bed for a deep sleep.

Anil had such a shock that he almost fainted. He had a complete blank look on his face. His mother happened to pass by his room. She called him to have tea but he didn't budge from his place. She entered his room and shook him thoroughly. He came out of his reverie.

She was scared to see his face which turned white due to the huge setback given by Monica. She asked him," What happened to you? I am your mother. Don't hide anything from me." Anil told her about Monica' s betrayal. She was so enraged that she felt like strangling Monica in person. She thought " How dare she give false hopes to my son and then dump him?" She controlled her emotions and consoled him saying, " Forget that girl. She is not fit to be my daughter in law. I will find a better match for you."

To her enormous surprise, he broke into tears. She had never seen him so upset, though heartbreak was not new for him. This time he was genuinely in love and his beloved had betrayed his trust. Anil wiped off his tears and asked his mother to prepare coffee for him. No sooner did she enter the kitchen, than the doorbell rang which was opened by

Anil. It was his best friend, Pramod who was grinning at him. Anil welcomed him with a bear hug. Both the friends exchanged pleasantries, sipping hot cups of coffee. Anil updated Pramod about his misfortune. He listened with rapt attention and appeared to be in a deep thought. He finally said, " If you have a portfolio of your work, just give it to me, I will ask Dad to help because he has a lot of business connections. I am sure he will be willing to help you." Anil cheered up considerably and fetched his portfolio. Pramod was very impressed with his work. He remarked, " Hey, You are an excellent artist and a great graphic designer. I am taking this with me. I will let you know by tomorrow."

Anil looked grateful. True to his word, Pramod called back, next morning stating that his dad was quite impressed with his work and wanted to talk to him in person. That was the turning point of his life. Pramod's father was a reputed businessman and had many business connections. Anil was asked to design a logo for a financial institution. He had come up with such a unique design, that it was immediately approved by the client. Gradually, more orders started pouring in for Anil. As a result, he set up his own advertising agency and started earning a lot through graphic design, animation and making portraits for art galleries.

He became a sort of celebrity, attracting international clients. He received the outstanding entrepreneur of the year award. He was on cloud nine, as his advertising agency raked in huge profits. He frequently travelled abroad. He made Pramod as his business partner and opened branches of his agency all over India, recruiting young talents. Vidya was proud of her son. Pramod' s younger sister, Niharika was attracted to him. She was a slim brunette of 20 having an oval face with doe shaped blue eyes, aquiline nose and rosy lips. She was absolutely gorgeous. Anil tried to avoid her because of his bad experience but finally gave in when Pramod and his father approved their marriage. The marriage was celebrated with much fanfare and many socialites graced the occasion. Anil had everything he had longed for, a beautiful wife, his own company, a mansion and several cars. His most prized possession was his best friend and brother in law Pramod, to whom he always remained grateful.

A fortnight after the marriage, he received a call from Monica. He disconnected and switched off his mobile. When he opened his email, he noticed several messages from Monica. They were full of apologies. She had mentioned that her wedding was called off by the groom. She stated that she had always regretted her decision and now that she is single, she wanted to marry him. He ignored and deleted all her messages. He was vexed with her relentless pursuit. He heard a rap at the door and looked up at Inspector Ravi, one of his college mate.

"Hello, My dearest friend! First of all let me congratulate you for your marriage. And secondly, I need your help with a case , that is if you are not too busy." " I am never too busy for my friends," Anil replied, " What can I do for you?" His friend answered, " There is an interesting case of online swindling by a girl. She hooks guys through website, promises to marry them and siphons off their bank balance. The unsuspecting guys fall for her charm and splurge all their money on her, only to be deserted in the end. I want you to draw her sketch because one of our artist is on leave and the complainant is coming tomorrow to our police station at 9.30 A.M. Will you come tomorrow?" Anil was intrigued. He agreed to come and then two friends parted ways.

Next morning, Anil reached Civil Lines Police Station by 9.15 A.M, where Ravi was posted as an inspector. The complainant Kishore was a friend of Ravi's brother Ajit.

Ravi asked him to narrate his ordeal once more before proceeding with the sketch. Anil asked him, " Have you personally met her?" Kishore said, "We had dated for a couple of months, before she broke up with me." Anil queried, "Don't you have any photos, that you may have taken together?

He answered, " This may sound weird but she never allowed me to take pictures together. I should have smelt something fishy about her behaviour."

Anil felt sorry for him. Without further questions, he took his drawing pad and pencil and started sketching based on the facial description given Kishore. It took more than an hour to complete the picture. When he finished the sketch, Anil glanced at it. The face seemed vaguely familiar. He showed the sketch to Kishore who confirmed that this was the same girl who had cheated him.

Anil tried to recall where he had seen her and then suddenly it all came to him in a flash. His face flushed with excitement. He added this photo on the computer and using his expertise in graphics and animation, made some alterations to her face and voila ! He grinned at Ravi and said, " Go and get your handcuffs ready, I know this bitch."

" How do you know her?" Ravi asked, unable to contain his excitement. Anil looked at both Kishore and Ravi. Then he told them all about her. They watched him with open mouth.

Anil returned home. He was in a jubilant mood. His wife Niharika and mother Vidya were amused to see him dancing like an overexcited kid. He explained them every thing. He put forth his plan to capture the online date fraud before them. They approved it. " Get ready, sweetheart! We will be going to our honeymoon to Darjeeling after our work in Kolkata is over."

He made a phone call and chatted on for a while. After disconnecting the call, he gave a thumbs up sign to his wife. She smiled and went away for packing their clothes for the trip. As per the plan, Ravi and a couple of police officers were supposed to hide at a safe place till Anil signalled them.

Two days later, Anil was dressed in a tuxedo and carried a bouquet. He had arrived at ' The Paradise café'. He was so handsome that some girls seated near the entrance found him irresistible and made a pass at him, much to Niharika' s annoyance. He slowly approached a girl with shiny, black hair that she had let open and which reached her slim waist. She was pretty, though not as beautiful as Niharika. He gave her the bouquet and she beamed at him. She began twirling the strands of her hair and gave him a seductive glance. She came near him and was about to kiss him but he stopped her and remarked, " Hold your horses, young lady. I would like you to meet some one special." Niharika came out of hiding. He introduced her to the girl, " Well, meet my wife Niharika ," he said and turned to his wife saying , " Niharika, meet Monica, the former love of my life. She is not only pretty but also wily enough to lure wealthy young men into her trap and once she robs them, she pretends fake marriage and proceeds to her next victim. By the way, I would like to know your real name. Is it Monica, Rushali , Jennifer or Fatima?"

Monica was stunned. Beads of perspiration formed in her forehead. She took a step back and tried to flee but unfortunately, the police came out of their hiding place and arrested her. " Your game is up." Ravi said and thanked Anil for his help. Anil shook hands with Ravi and then left with his wife for the honeymoon

TWO

An orphan girl, who grew up in an orphanage. He passed tenth and got a private job. And started doing further studies together. A single girl who has neither father nor brother nor sister. That lonely girl and her loneliness. Six days of the week he used to go out for school and office work, one Sunday was left, he would go out in some rest. There was no happiness and no sorrow to ask for pain. Putting his head on whose shoulder in sorrow, narrating his pain, who would tell him about this bad society and the customs of the society. She went to another city for further studies. started living there. Started doing private part time job. His routine, working six days a week at office and college, "was just in his first year of graduation. She used to live alone from the first step of her teenage years. where that girl lived. After a few days there, a boy came to live in the neighborhood. For some time he did not know that someone lived in a nearby room. But often she used to go to the office. This went on for several days. Later one day the boy asked for his mobile number. The boy gave his mobile number and started talking. Both were strangers in that stranger city. The girl started talking because she was an orphan. Initially, good friends were talking, the girl also started giving more time to talk, that handsome boy brought a motorcycle after five-six months. They both started going for walks often. One day the boy expressed his love to her and promised that "I will marry you" The girl believed it and kissed her on the lips. Both started coming very close.

One day the boy took her out for a walk. Then took him to a hotel. There she was raped and handed over to his friends. In this way he betrays her. The girl made friendship as a true life partner, but the boy betrayed her, betrayed her. The poor girl who had lost everything. Who would teach him, the society in this bad, about bad works, about good and bad, to differentiate. Because neither was his father, who would protect him. Neither is his mother who makes him cultured. Similarly, he did not have a brother who would protect him, nor a sister who would have been his support at the age of that age. What he considered to be a support turned out to be a scoundrel. The girl who wants to settle down with him. Wanting to give her everything she wants to do with him, "together with her friends" the girl, who was a poor orphan destitute. One of his greatest jewels, which was respect, was mixed in the soil. When that girl found out, it was too late. spoiled that girl's life. The girl came to her room with him, thinking about herself. While coming, he thought of dying, but the cruelty that his friend had done to him. His friend's friends, who had now ruined his life. Wanted to teach him a lesson. Because what happened to me should not happen to anyone else. But what could have happened even by writing a sentence? He made up his mind that from now on, this should not happen to any girl. He worked hard for a long time and formed an organization, which would show the right path to the destitute and orphan girl. To save her from a wrong decision made at the time of her ignorant age, she started to make them aware and to punish those who did the same thing with her. Strengthened his organization, together he knew that even the law cannot do anything in such cases without evidence.

THREE

One day Georgina received a friend request from a serviceman on peacekeeping duties in Afghanistan. She decided to accept the request and allowed 'Jim' to be her Facebook friend. It didn't start as a romance but he said he was lonely and looking for friends to keep him company while he was stuck on duty in the middle of nowhere. Soon after befriending her, Jim told Georgina he had lost his wife to cancer and his story of looking after her was similar to her own experience when her husband had died of cancer.

'He then said he was being posted to Nigeria but his time in the U.S military was nearly finished. He sent me pictures which I now know were stolen from someone on the internet. He kept saying he couldn't wait for us to be together. We became very close and he emailed me every day saying it was easier for him than using Facebook.'

Jim, who was a scammer, told Georgina he liked gemstones and wanted to set up a jewellery store when he retired. He said this was the best part of being in Nigeria because it was close to where the precious stones were being mined and he could buy them very cheaply.

He told Georgina he was coming to see her but had some trouble with his bank card not working in Nigeria and couldn't get funds to pay for an export tax on his gemstones. Georgina transferred some money to him to cover the tax which he explained was only two per cent of the value of the gemstones but still amounted to $15 000. It was a lot of money to send but she figured he was a good and honest serviceman and if things worked out they would spend the rest of their lives together.

'All was going well until his stopover in Malaysia. Customs officials seized the gemstones and demanded payment to have them released. This time they were asking $20 000. I told him it would take some time to get the money and I had to borrow against the family home.'

Georgina sent the money to Malaysian officials but was told Jim was now in gaol for smuggling and that she needed to contact his lawyer.

'The lawyer said he needed to get an Anti-terrorism and Money Laundering certificate and this would be another $10 000. He said he also needed to pay for Jim's court costs plus his own fees and this would be another $5000.'

Georgina sent the money but then Jim said there was another government official demanding payment to extend his visa while he waited for the court to process all the documents.

'Almost every day I was contacted with a new demand for money. They sent me certificates signed by officials, forms to fill out and bills for everything. If you wanted to get anything done quickly you had to pay another fee. It seemed to me that the whole Malaysian government was corrupt. I don't know exactly how much money I sent but it was well over $100 000. I didn't care about the money. I just wanted to help Jim and I honestly thought he would pay me back.'

Even when Georgina ran out of money the demands didn't stop. Unsure of what to do, Georgina finally talked to the police. They explained that her experience included the common features of a dating and romance scam and it would be very unlikely she would get her money back. She can't help feeling in her heart that she let Jim down but she knows in her head it was all a scam.

● 27 ●

FOUR

Sometimes love makes life and sometimes it makes life hell.... We do not see hell with our eyes hell is just our imagination and nothing else...... Hell is a place where nobody wants to live ...... According to our knowledge, hell and heaven will a lot to a person after death in the light of his or her sins or good deeds but some people have to survive in hell during their lifetime.....

The hero of my story is also surviving in hell during his lifetime... Here is my story....

He entered in his university, met his friends and then saw a very beautiful girl and he continuously looking at her without blinking his eyes.... He asked his friends that who is this girl his friend told him that she is new comer here and her name is Ayesha..... He was play boy type personality and he was a bunch of girl friends but that girl makes him mad..... He left all his negative habits for her and then follow her. Girl becomes irritated when any boy comes close to the girl he starts beating him....

Finally girl stopped him and asked what's your problem, what do you want and the boy straight forwardly said that I LOVE YOU AYESHA AND I WANT YOU IN MY LIFE AS MY LIFE PARTNER... Girl starts laughing and said try this to another girl I know your history and I know you never loves someone. Boy starts weeping and said I really love you this happens first time in my life and I am also surprised about this. Tell me how I can prove my love and sincerity towards you...

Ayesha replied: give your life but don't irritate me and follow me. He said ok and then he go away. About two to three days she does not see that boy and then she asked his cousin that where is arsh? She told her that he is in hospital he is very serious he had an accident..... She became worried and goes to hospital to see him. He was in conscious state and asked Ayesha that are you satisfied now? Ayesha slapped him and scolds him.

Finally, he thought that he got his love and then became very happy. They spend all the time together and time was very good for both.... But bad time was also waiting for him... one day he received an mms on his phone and that mms broke him. That mms contains naked pictures of Ayesha with a boy. He did not say a single word to Ayesha and quietly facing everything. That incident was finishing him from inside.

And then he received a call that come to this address and saw your Ayesha in somebody's arms. He reached there and saw Ayesha with a boy on bed. He shouted and told Ayesha about that mms. Ayesha asked him that she left him but can't stay away from him and come to meet him for the last time. Arsh become angry and start weeping and get out a pistol from his pocket and said Ayesha I loved you a lot but you deceive me stay with your love and be happy forever never play with anyone's feelings again and shoot on his temple and died......

FIVE

www.ingramcontent.com/pod-product-compliance
Lightning Source LLC
Chambersburg PA
CBHW020944160726
47993CB00007B/2924